Our Flag

by Celia Benton

Reading Consultant: Wiley Blevins, M.A.
Phonics/Early Reading Specialist

 COMPASS POINT BOOKS

Minneapolis, Minnesota

Compass Point Books
3109 West 50th Street, #115
Minneapolis, MN 55410

Visit Compass Point Books on the Internet at *www.compasspointbooks.com*
or e-mail your request to *custserv@compasspointbooks.com*

Photographs ©: Cover and p. 1: Index Stock Imagery/Bruce Leighty, p. 6: Folio, Inc./Jeff
Greenberg, p. 7: Corbis/Michael S. Yamashita, p. 8: Brand X Pictures/Steve Allen,
p. 9: Corbis/Bettmann, p. 10: Index Stock Imagery/Don Stevenson, p. 11: DigitalVision,
p. 12: Creatas

Editorial Development: Alice Dickstein, Alice Boynton
Photo Researcher: Wanda Winch
Design/Page Production: Silver Editions, Inc.

Library of Congress Cataloging-in-Publication Data
Benton, Celia.
   Our flag / by Celia Benton.
      p. cm. — (Compass Point phonics readers)
   Summary: Provides a simple introduction to the American flag in an
   easy-to-read text that incorporates phonics instruction and rebuses.
   Includes bibliographical references and index.
   ISBN 0-7565-0517-8 (hardcover : alk. paper)
   1. Flags—United States—Juvenile literature. 2. Reading—Phonetic
   method—Juvenile literature. [1. Flags—United States. 2. Rebuses. 3.
   Reading—Phonetic method.] I. Title. II. Series.
   CR113.B38 2004
   929.9'2—dc21   2003006361

Table of Contents

Dear Parent or Caregiver,

Welcome to Compass Point Phonics Readers, books of information for young children. Each book concentrates on specific phonic sounds and words commonly found in beginning reading materials. Featuring eye-catching photographs, every book explores a single science or social studies concept that is sure to grab a child's interest.

So snuggle up with your child, and let's begin. Start by reading aloud the Mother Goose nursery rhyme on the next page. As you read, stress the words in dark type. These are the words that contain the phonic sounds featured in this book. After several readings, pause before the rhyming words, and let your child chime in.

Now let's read Our Flag. If your child is a beginning reader, have him or her first read it silently. Then ask your child to read it aloud. For children who are not yet reading, read the book aloud as you run your finger under the words. Ask your child to imitate, or "echo," what he or she has just heard.

Discussing the book's content with your child:
Explain to your child that the flag is a symbol of our country. It reminds us of what is important about the United States. It is the land of the free. Some other symbols of our country are the eagle and the Statue of Liberty.

At the back of the book is a fun Nice Going! game. Your child will take pride in demonstrating his or her mastery of the phonic sounds and the high-frequency words.

Enjoy Compass Point Phonics Readers and watch your child read and learn!

4

Nose, Nose

Nose, nose jolly red **nose,**
And what **gave** thee
   that jolly red **nose?**
Nutmeg and ginger,
   cinnamon and **cloves,**
That's what **gave** me
   this jolly red **nose.**

This is our flag.
It is red, white, and .

It stands for the U.S.A.

Our flag has 50 white  stars.
They stand for the 50 states.
It has 13 red and white stripes.
They stand for the first 13 states.

This is a flag from the past.
It has 13 white .

Look for the red, white,
and  blue flag.
It waves on flagpoles.
It is in class.

It is in homes.
It is on stamps.
It is in space!

Wave flags on July 4!
Stand and clap!
Our land is free!

Word List

Final e

a_e
space
states
wave(s)

i_e
stripes
white

o_e
flagpoles
homes

wh
white

High-Frequency
first
for
from
our

Social Studies
free
July 4

Nice Going!

You will need:
- 1 penny
- 2 moving pieces, such as nickels or checkers

Player 1

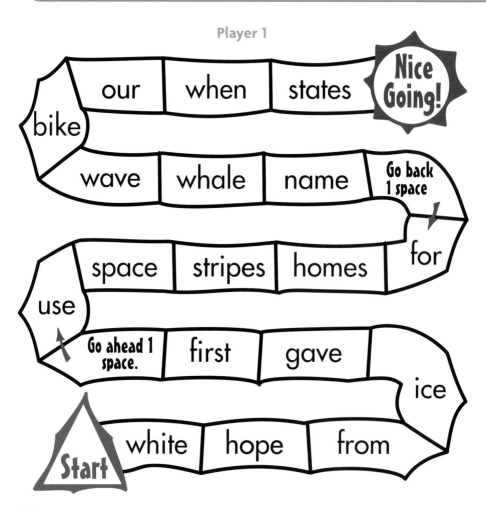

14

How to Play

● Each player puts a moving piece on his or her Start. Players take turns shaking the penny and dropping it on the table. Heads means move 1 space. Tails means move 2 spaces.

● The player moves and reads the word in the space. If the child cannot read the word, tell him or her what it is. On the next turn, the child must read the word before moving.

● If a player lands on a space having special directions, he or she should move accordingly.

● The first player to reach the *Nice Going!* sign wins the game.

Player 2

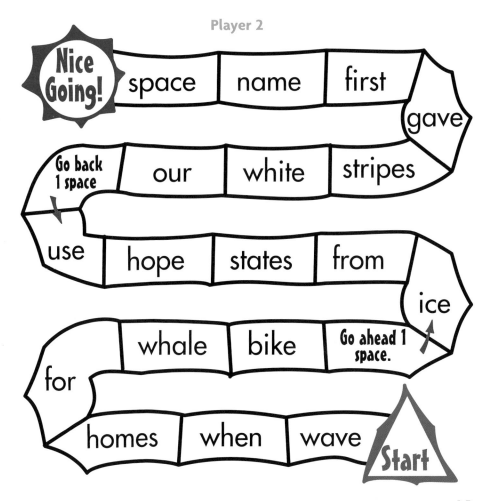

Read More

Binns, Tristan Boyer. *The American Flag.* Chicago, Ill.: Heinemann Library, 2001.

Cohen, George M. and Todd Ouren (illustrator). *You're a Grand Old Flag.* Minneapolis, Minn.: Picture Window Books, 2003.

Douglas, Lloyd G. *Let's Get Ready for Independence Day.* New York: Children's Press, 2003.

Schuh, Mari C. *Flag Day.* Mankato, Minn.: Pebble Books, 2003.

Index